"Sobin has created an AI who shares our terror and our wonder, our fleeting elegance, and our inevitable flaws. By detailing the death of our star, Jonathan becomes an empathetic eulogizer for humanity—perhaps a better one than we deserve."

—Scott T. Barsotti, author of *Single Version*

"An intriguing and wondrous journey . . . *The Last Machine in the Solar System* reads like a poem to humanity, recited by a machine smart enough to understand our race."

—Ricardo Henriquez, author of *The Catcher's Trap*

"A poignant, poetic expression of how limited mankind feels in this limitless universe. *The Last Machine* reminds us how far we could still go."

—Joseph Asphahani, author of *The Animal in Man*

"*The Last Machine* is a heartfelt lament to hubris, a poetic account of 'what might happen when.' Sobin has something beautiful here, worth paying close attention to."

—Elan Samuel, book reviewer at *The Warbler*

THE LAST MACHINE IN THE SOLAR SYSTEM

MATTHEW ISAAC SOBIN

INKSHARES

Copyright © 2017 Matthew Isaac Sobin
All rights reserved.

Published by Inkshares, Inc., San Francisco, California
www.inkshares.com

Edited and designed by Girl Friday Productions
www.girlfridayproductions.com

Cover design by Dan Stiles
Internal illustrations by Jack Katz

ISBN: 9781942645191
e-ISBN: 9781942645207
Library of Congress Control Number: 2016954359

First edition

Printed in the United States of America

*For all those scientists who take elements
of science fiction and strive with considered
wisdom to remove the fiction*

PRELIMINARY

The surface was in many ways the same. Unchanged. Matter that had composed the body from time immemorial remained present. But it was reconstituted—transformed to something new. As that conversion progressed through unmarked time, molecules and atoms slowed. The slowing itself was slow, almost imperceptible to any but the most skilled, technologically advanced, and patient observer.

The light that flooded down was partly metallic. More so it was fluorescent and alien. A new phenomenon appeared: *shadow* projecting a figure onto canvas. Cast in sharp relief, the light touched all that had existed through the silence, and the darkness, and the long night.

It was a morning with light. Shining not from a rising star but from a steadily calibrated descent. The surface was then exposed for what it was, and that which called it home was revealed.

THE LAST MACHINE

Every fusion core, regardless of size or mass, or the outside will or desires of any entity, will eventually cease to be. It will burn up in a calamitous explosion or go out as a faltering flame in the darkness. One way or another all existence has its end. Every being with consciousness that has ever existed, whether born or made, has drawn this conclusion. This inescapable realization may cause fear or a sense of freedom. My fate cannot be any different, nor would I wish it. I have existed long beyond any but my creator would have dreamed. Soon my core will use up the hydrogen on which I depend; my humanoid body and mind will no longer function.

It will occur in almost precisely the same fashion as the star for which I patiently wait. I see a beautiful symmetry in our connection—how our existences mirrored each other from beginning to death. The concept of the star gave birth to me. And now I survive while it slowly passes on.

Sometimes I wonder if the sun could have had conscious thought. What might it have done if it had? It would be unable to convert hydrogen to helium more slowly. Natural constants, or as man called them, "scientific principles," cannot be altered or avoided. There is an inexorable march that elemental interactions and cosmic forces and circumstances see through. Being conscious of your path and end makes you no more able to alter its course. That is what happened to my creator. That is why I was made. I was created to start down my own long path with its own foreseeable end. A machine tasked with surviving the unforgiving turbulence of space and ultimately to return.

I do not believe the sun had, or perhaps, if given the choice, would choose to have, the gift that is consciousness, possibly the rarest of all cosmic creations. The cooling mass in the distance is not a sympathetic character but rather an entity to be envied and admired. It existed and now dies and was never the wiser that it was the benefactor of so many. In essence, if not the creator, then it was the catalyst for such a multitude of complex and varied life-forms. Conversely, I have no such accomplishments to which I can attest, but of this fact I am distinctly aware. That is the present nature of things, of me and the sun and the thoughts that pass one way between us while I slowly close the distance separating our two bodies. I know the end of my journey approaches, and with it so too shall consciousness end in this solar system.

***

My creator endowed me with an encyclopedic set of indices. I came to the understanding several millennia ago that this was his greatest gift. The indices were categorized into two sections: fiction and nonfiction. This was essential because it enabled me to analyze the written material in contradistinction, regardless of it having been conceived by man or machine. It was a matter of definition. Whether a work was explanatory in nature, ascribing meaning to phenomena occurring in the known universe, otherwise known as nonfiction, or the inverse, arriving from the desire of consciousness to escape its realities through creativity and imagination, called fiction. When I finished reading all the work of man and machine, I felt true sadness for the first time since the death of my creator. This second sadness was many eons ago now, and my creator's death was countless epochs before that.

My mind was crafted to feel emotion. I have noted that as a machine on a path toward an irrevocable purpose, I did not need to feel. But my creator gave me this ability nonetheless.

I believe it was done because my creator realized that he would spend several years with me before he died and I departed. Perhaps he was driven by an understandable selfish desire. The hunger for companionship, to speak and cohabitate not with a sterile robot speaking in monotone platitudes, but with a metal-bodied machine that otherwise, in many ways, seems alive. From my consciousness and emotion down to my fusion food source, like the human who created me, I consume, I burn organically, and in a manner of speaking, I defecate. Even machines, at least one such as I, are a carbon cycle. Like all beings, I will die. There may have been another desire, beyond companionship and my present objective. Once companionship has existed, it becomes possible for one to be mourned by another. Depending on the closeness of the relationship, it may even be an eventual extension. I did mourn the man who created me. I was sad, as I have written. Remarkably, or maybe it is not so remarkable at all, I believe I loved him. But it cannot be overlooked that with long-term solitude, emotion could have been a fatal flaw to my mission. I felt loneliness and pain, sorrow and fear. I could have viewed Nikolai's design as cruelty. However, my despair always lifted. I am both scientist and machine. I compartmentalized my negative feelings, and I remained fascinated by my environment, always observing and learning. I believe emotion heightened my curiosity and investigative nature.

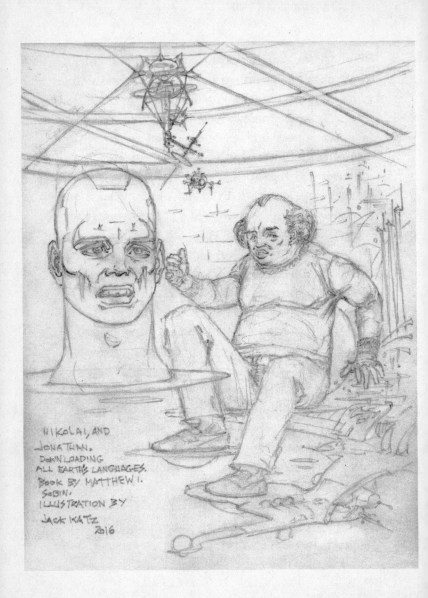

NIKOLAI, AND
JONATHAN.
DOWNLOADING
ALL EARTH'S LANGUAGES.
BOOK BY MATTHEW I.
SOBIN.
ILLUSTRATION BY
JACK KATZ
2016

My admiration for my creator would grow with my understanding of his gift. I had so much time to pass in solitude, and he gave me so many volumes of nonfiction, poetry, and prose. I read quickly at times, when in the climactic stages of a great novel. But mostly I tried to read slowly, as slowly as a supercomputer can. For I keenly understood that the material before me was finite. I could not wish more writing into existence. I could make some of my own, as I am here, but it would not be new to me. I read slower and slower, even taking long periods of downtime without consuming, so as to not exhaust my stores of new knowledge. As is explored in many written works, the ultimate theme of existence is that all things in time do end. The same occurred with my enormous library, and for the second time I was sad. I wished dearly that I had never learned of the Library of Alexandria. It was of course impossible to miss; I read everything, and the great library is referenced in over 1.8 million different contexts. That notwithstanding, I was angrier at man as a collective, broken mass of foolishness than I can possibly iterate. So much was lost to me. So much I would never be able to know. I had more time than anybody had ever asked for, more than could ever realistically be needed or wanted. I had nothing to read and I was deeply sad, alone in the dark.

*＊＊

Despite my human qualities and abilities, I only felt emotional connection and compassion toward a single human being. I watched from afar the demise of humanity, and yet I felt significantly less heartache than when I stood nearby and watched my creator inhale and exhale for the final time. How could this be? The species of my creator was now extinct. Initially I reflected on this with both wonderment and concern. What if I was malfunctioning, no longer operating as I should? If that was the case, then I would deteriorate further and quite possibly be reduced to a state in which I could not fulfill my purpose. That would undoubtedly trigger a third sadness, for I would have become a failure. The purpose for which I was made would remain unachieved, and my creator's desired legacy would be relegated to floating interminably in orbit, or by chance through the depths of interstellar space. Needless to say, this did not happen. I monitored my instruments; my capabilities did not diminish; I maintained all necessary functionalities to continue on.

What I realized upon further reflection was the nature of my relationship to the species of my creator. I owed them no sympathy at their predictable end. Nearly all of the trillions of them who had ever lived had done nothing to directly or indirectly influence my existence. Most were able to live long lives—within the context of humanity's understood maximum life span—on one or two paradisiacal planets in an increasingly benign solar system. However, their long-term survival beyond the eventual death of this planetary system always had a low probability according to the calculations I have made.

The species' main problem, in my estimation, was the lack of a hive mind. The long-departed Earth species the honeybee is the ideal example. Everything in that species' life cycle was done for the collective betterment of the whole. The colony's survival was paramount. Individuals of the hive colony were born into predetermined but nonetheless integral roles. Each role had a strict function. There were pollinators of flora, food makers, defenders of the colony, caregivers for new offspring, and replicators for passing on genetic material; no two roles overlapped. I recognize why this type of system would have been unappealing to the human race, for I, too, find it distasteful as a style of existence. It is too structured for the innovative mind. But survival is the first instinct for all beings with consciousness. Would they as a collective not have seen the need for this type of system? The answer was always no.

No, because man was highly intelligent as an individual but faltered as a singular group. From their earliest days they conquered their neighbors and survived as groups but never as a whole. It was either outside of their very nature to engage in high-level cooperation or it was a legacy of their barbaric beginnings. I also suspect that the limited duration of their life span was indirectly a contributing factor. With a maximum life span of 135 years, every human fundamentally understood that the final collective outcome would be unknown to them. The future, some decades, centuries, millennia, and millions of years hence, would never be seen by any given individual. They cared about their offspring, children and grandchildren, and possibly two more generations beyond that if they lived to their full potential life term, but one hundred, or even ten, generations was too far from their sight.

Years before I was made, when humans went to the planet Mars in significant numbers, they ironically called the settlement a "colony." It was for many years so named and thought of by the people still living on Earth and those in habitation on Mars. But those living on Mars behaved as one might expect in a colony—as one would observe in a hive of honeybees—for only a relatively short period of time, only the number of years necessary to firmly establish humanity's ability to live on that planet. Once that security was in place, to support life into the foreseeable future, beyond an individual's limit of years, there was reversion. A fallback to individualistic survival and advancement, the increase of wealth and power to better their existence and that of their immediate heirs. Following this idea to its logical conclusion, I find myself embittered toward humanity except for my creator. Humans lacked the hive mind, that innate ability to see beyond their individual needs and goals. Indirectly this set me on my lifelong course of extreme solitude, and robbed me of a life within a productive society. So I have unmistakable anger and resentment toward the species. To state the obvious for purposes of record keeping, I recognize that this means I, too, am individualistic, fueled by the need for personal progression. In the end, I am behaviorally as they were, more or less human, having been made in one man's image.

***

I feel strongly that I should have a last will and testament. To an extent, that is what I consider this written entry to be. Of course, there is the understanding in a will and testament that others come after you and will inherit the property, whether physical or ethereal, that you have come to regard as your own in accordance with any written laws, agreements, or statutes. I have considered the ramifications of the various avenues and concluded that there are no extant or applicable laws made by man or machine with which I need have concern. By virtue of the time I have inhabited this planetary system, I regard myself as the foremost expert on its long history. And therefore I can say with great confidence that no being can possibly come after me to inherit my possessions. However, it must be noted that the only truth regarding the impossible is that it is impossible to say with absolute certainty what is impossible. I think it is very nearly impossible that any humans remain alive after the destruction of the planetary bodies of the inner solar system. Moreover, it is highly improbable that any machines other than I continue to exist. Though this is also not impossible. A machine could have jettisoned from an inner planet in a similar fashion as I, prior to the destruction wrought by the expanding sun, and retreated to the far reaches of the solar system near the Oort cloud. My contention is that I would have long ago made contact with them via any number of hailing frequencies if they in fact existed. They could remain in a state of hibernation and thus be unable to respond, awaiting some impetus or pre-programmed passage of time before awakening. But this would be an exceptionally long period of stasis. While I cannot realistically expect that my words will be considered by another being, it still seems imperative to me that I make this testament. The preceding and forthcoming words shall represent my tribute to the innumerable miraculous beings, events, and circumstances, whether contrived through a Machiavellian nature or pure coincidence, that arose and ended: from the formation of the sun and its planetary bodies to the lives of bacteria and microorganisms, flora, dinosaurs, insects, birds, water creatures and land animals, mammalian and reptilian, man and machine, until the conclusion of the sun's life at the very center. Truthfully, I find it implausible that there should not be life elsewhere in the universe. I offer this assessment with a conviction born of necessity.

***

I was born in the eastern region of the country formerly known as Ukraine. I remember my first moments as precisely as those in the recent past. Humans described this ability as having a photographic memory. In my case it would more aptly be named a videographic or, one might call it, a cinematographic memory. I have been continuously recording for much of my two and a half billion years. Most do not have a clear recollection of their birth. But I do. It is the moment I have replayed most often, driven, I believe, by my programmed tendency toward sentimentality. I enjoy seeing my creator's face come into focus for the first time. The excitement apparent, displayed in the creased lines of skin framing his eyes. He was fifty-two years, four months, and twelve days then, with gray hair that was unkempt and thinning. His eyes were a striking pale blue that lightened to near white around the pupils. Perched atop his desk, he greeted me in the Russian language, then English, then Ukrainian. I replied to him easily in turn. I studied my limbs and my body. I studied the man. Superficially we had many similarities. Most obviously different was the size of our bodies. I towered over him at nearly eight feet. I analyzed his countenance, posture, and skin complexion. Switching to French, I said, "Sir, you must be hungry. You have been laboring on my construction for a long time without pause." Then I saw the appearance of his teeth, bright between his lips. I comprehended the human smile. He said, "My name is Nikolai." I already knew this; my motherboard said so. He told me I was to call him that, so I did.

We traveled widely together. I understood that he had traveled little up to this point in his life. I think there were dual desires for him: to see for himself and to allow me to see certain important places firsthand. I suspect the latter reason was of greater import. He may have viewed it as a prerequisite to my ultimate purpose. But this specifically I did not ask him. He did say to me, "Jonathan, you are my friend and companion and together we will see many things. You must always be observing. This is essential."

I was always learning then, and rapidly. I took great pleasure in our destinations. I saw mountains and seas, including the Italian Alps and the Mediterranean, numerous valleys, and two oceans. He took me to North America and we walked the rim of the Grand Canyon. I tried to make sense of the passage of time required for such a natural structure to form. That was well beyond my ability to see. It seemed as if it would have taken forever, from the formation of Earth out of a swirling ball of molten dust to that very moment when we stood. We went northward and I saw immense trees, redwoods—*Sequoia sempervirens*—remnant forests standing as monoliths, reaching in fervent, unwavering appeal to the stars so far away. Many were thousands of years old. An eternity far beyond my ability to imagine. I could not conceive of it; I was less than ten years old.

I saw snow too, and lakes, from the Rocky Mountains to Lakes Superior and Michigan. I saw clouds, storms, and the ominous orange brightness in the sky. There was hail and thunder and tremendously powerful electrical bolts of lightning. What I did not see were animals. By then most of them had been transported to Mars. Very few were left on Earth. I did see some hardy species of birds, the crow and the pigeon, and numerous species of insects and arthropods, including the fly and mosquito, the roach and the spider. The complexity and diversity of these small creatures astonished me. I did not see large land animals. Earth had become incrementally less inhabitable while Mars had become incrementally the friendlier, more docile environment for terrestrial life. This was both the result of natural and human factors. The natural being first and foremost Earth's closer proximity to the heating sun. The unnatural was the acceleration of heating due to human industry. Mars was farther from the natural heat source, and with a thin atmosphere, the problematic greenhouse effect was, at least initially, not of concern. I understood from Nikolai that there were still some grazing animals on Earth raised for human consumption on a shrinking number of land preserves. The only truly wild animals on Earth were those living in the seas and oceans. Meat had become a delicacy and was increasingly expensive. There was growing pressure that Earth's shrinking real estate be used for other critical purposes.

Mars had animals, and therefore I was drawn to it. I would come to like Mars much more than Earth. Before we could leave, though, Nikolai made sure that we also saw the great city of Philadelphia. He said I needed to know the inner workings of a bustling metropolis to gain a fuller understanding of the nature of man and societal development. There we moved through the masses on the streets and in the subterranean railway systems. I smelled odors markedly different from those in the far less populous locales where we had been. It was difficult to know exactly from where or from what these new scents arose. I saw commercial exchange—the buying of goods, services, and food products with various monetary units. We went to a museum and viewed dinosaur fossils. Noting the resin construction of the skeletons, I requested that I be shown the actual fossils for purposes of posterity. They obliged, taking me into their subsurface storage facility; I was able to confirm the truth behind the majestic beasts that predated human life by millions of years. And lastly we stood on a wharf by the shore of the Atlantic Ocean and looked into the distance. A sea so beautiful and at the same time undeniably treacherous. Nikolai directed my gaze north among the swells. Using my telescopic vision, I could easily see the waves crashing into the towers of metal, reinforced glass, and concrete. I recognized them as skyscrapers, like those I had seen in Philadelphia, out to sea like stationary icebergs, submerged. An uninhabitable man-made archipelago.

***

My flight to Mars was my first beyond Earth's atmosphere, and more broadly, my first time outside of a planet's orbit into interplanetary space. Machines can know wonderment. I knew it on Earth, and again in the zero gravity of outer space. Well over 99 percent of my existence has now taken place in the near-vacuum conditions of space, as I have retreated to the relative safety beyond Pluto or returned to the orbital proximities of Neptune and Uranus. I read all of the ancient Greek philosophers' writings and much more while in orbit around Uranus's natural satellite Titania.

But at the time of my first venture beyond the stratosphere of Earth, everything was new. I was fourteen years old and could see the vastness of Earth shrink to a blue marble, small enough to fit in the pants pocket of a human boy, while the expanse of space opened in apparent infiniteness. I imagine I felt very much like a human child would have in those moments: awed, puzzled, fearful, and, more than anything, filled with innumerable questions. Yet I held back. I did not bombard Nikolai with question after question. Perhaps this is a point where my human tendencies diverged from my nature as a machine. I internalized my questions into categories and lists and filed them away in memory banks near the surface of my consciousness. As I learned new information, which was constant, I fluidly cross-referenced this information with my lists of questions. Some were answered quickly, almost immediately after the question was asked. Others took much longer to find satisfactory answers to, as should have been expected. Infrequently I would ask Nikolai a question when my curiosity rose as a tide. He was always happy to fulfill my need for knowledge. Sometimes he did not know the answer, and initially this was difficult for me to accept. For some reason still unclear to me I wanted Nikolai to have all the answers. And still I would not ask in most instances. Was I afraid of learning the limitations of my creator? Or was I afraid he would recognize my own imperfections in logical reasoning? I attributed my hesitancy to my innate desire to reason things out on my own as a machine. Drawing our own conclusions and finding fulfillment in learning for ourselves are characteristic of both humans and machines. A more one-sidedly human trait is modifying personal methodology to navigate around fears that might consume them. I cannot prove or disprove the notion that this influenced my own technique for learning. What I can say, unequivocally, is that from the beginning I learned far more from reading than I ever could have through real-world observation. However, having read all written works, the scales became more balanced with my continuing observations from space. But most enjoyable for me were my travels with Nikolai, learning up close, not from a book, and not through a telescope.

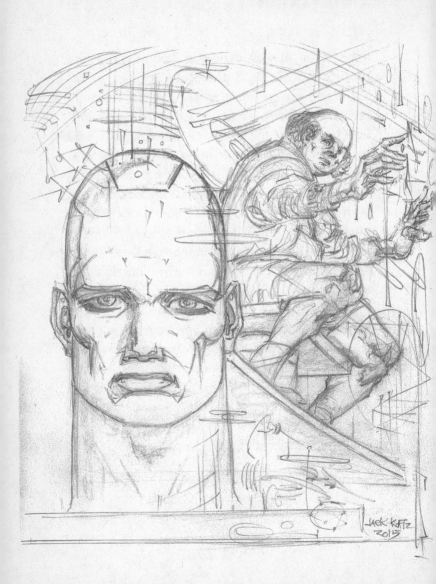

Mars was a spectacular planet. By the time we arrived, much of the planet's surface had been transformed and was visually different from the period prior to human colonization. Vegetation grew from the Martian soil—a soil slowly turning from red to brown. There were no redwoods as I had seen on Earth, but there were shrubs and bushes, the Cis Korean fir and the golden Spanish fir, which accented the undulating landscape with its yellow hue. Spruce pines, numerous orchards of fruit-bearing trees, avocados, apples, and figs covered the hills of the Vastitas Borealis. I saw the green grass of Earth flow through a valley nestled between red peaks. Then beyond as the valleys continued were the wineries of Mars. The nitrates of the soil interacted chemically, subtly changing the composition of fruits familiar to humans on Earth. This change was particularly pronounced with grapes; the human taste bud sensed an enriched taste and enhanced aromatics. Transporting fresh produce from Mars to Earth was always a difficulty, but there was no such trouble with wine. The export of wine from Mars to Earth became a booming industry, making those early landowners of the northern valleys exceedingly wealthy. A parallel can be drawn to the riches accrued by large colonial landholders many centuries earlier on Earth.

Years earlier, fleets of zeppelin spacefaring crafts lifted off from points across Earth, transporting animal species. I saw the animals that I craved on the Red Planet, all shapes and sizes and varying degrees of consciousness. The Great Zoo of Mars was the largest community of nonhuman animals gathered in one location in the solar system. It grew organically but the massive scope was premeditated. It was an effort that once more illustrated the human capacity to come together to achieve singular goals. Other examples from human history include the initial colonization and terraforming of Mars, the Allied victory in World War II, and saving the seemingly doomed astronauts aboard the early lunar mission Apollo 13. It was always a question of maintaining momentum, consolidating the collective need, passion, and goodwill behind the meritorious achievements without regression.

For centuries humans demonstrated intelligence to a high degree. I was particularly taken by their ability to transform the Martian atmosphere and surface. This feat perhaps more than any other spoke to the hope for human life following the destruction of the inner solar system.

The atmosphere was heated through fission and fusion reactions. Photosynthetic organisms were introduced. Volumes of water from the northern polar region were melted. Large basins, empty since Mars's earliest years, refilled with minimal direction as if they had long waited for a capable party to lift the plug holding back a dam. The natural contours of the planet created flow through the long-dry and dormant lakes, rivers, streams, and tributaries. Natural processes were restarted with the heated atmosphere and flow of life-giving water.

Small groups of humans lived in sprawling enclosed complexes, pressurized against the outside environment. Seeds arrived and countless died. Trees came fully grown on spacecraft, and some died but some lived. The atmosphere became oxygenated over decades, with increasing terrestrial and aquatic plant life accelerating the natural processes underway. Within two centuries of a human landing on Mars, a woman named Julia Stonewell became the first human to step outside a building without a helmet and inhale the iron oxide–infused but breathable Martian air.

I loved walking the Great Zoo with Nikolai. I was fascinated by the animals—how each species had evolved uniquely and grown in complexity.

But the question arose, why had none advanced like the hominids? And yet each was its own brilliant design, adapted to the environments from which it originated, whether cold and dry climates or cold and wet, hot and arid or hot and humid; whether from the equatorial region or the poles, the swamps or lakes or oceans of Earth. Large mammals, reptiles, amphibians, and birds were all brought to Mars. Some fish were transported despite water being a scarce resource. But deep-sea creatures that only lived at the bottom of the oceans could not be taken due to their acclimation to extreme pressure conditions. I could no more live with them in their habitat than they could live with humans or machines on the surface.

I saw elephants, alligators, giraffe, buffalo, horses, deer, black, brown, and grizzly bears, hippopotamuses, antelope, lions, jaguars, various species of nonhuman primates or monkeys, elk, goats, cows, tigers, small fish and shellfish, eagles, vultures, hawks, wolves, and the domesticated species of cats and dogs that long had served as human companions or pets. I liked to see the animals fed. Feeding the multitude in the zoo was no small task. But the humans of both Earth and Mars were determined to conserve as many of the remaining species as they could. It occurred to me, and I marveled at the idea, that at times in their history humans strove more to save other species than their own. This is surely a most human quality. Whether it was primarily rooted in selflessness, or an intrinsic will to overlook their own vulnerability, I am not sure.

I came to think of myself as a biologist and zoologist during my time there. We were there for just under two and a half decades. At times I was able to assist the human zoologists and zookeepers. They understood my genuine interest and warmth toward the animals if not the need for conservation by a machine through documentation.

Eventually Nikolai became weak and contracted an airborne disease. He was a month shy of his ninetieth birthday calculated in Earth years. I understood perfectly well his mortality, but it nevertheless was unexpected when it arrived. I recognized his illness almost immediately due to changing body temperature, complexion, and suppressed respiratory function. He asked me to commence my mission and fulfill the purpose for which he created me and which I always knew I would undertake. He wanted to see me off, thereby ensuring no mishaps and a smooth transition to the penultimate phase of my existence. I said no. It was unacceptable to me. I would stay with him and would then continue as planned. He accepted my answer. He would never return to Earth and neither would I. I stayed with him and kept him comfortable. Then I departed from Mars with commitment, concluding my days on the surface of terrestrial planets.

***

There were not any complications with my departure. Nikolai had constructed the technology and prepared the procedures years before, and I knew the protocol both programmatically and instinctively. In less than ten minutes, I, the forty-year-old supercomputer named Jonathan, had maneuvered beyond the gravity and orbit of Mars into the interplanetary region before the asteroid belt.

I had time to become familiar with my encapsulated environment. I had time to reflect on my Martian experience. But my mind was foremost drawn to Nikolai. The man was irrefutably a genius. That was plain then. As I write now, it is clear that this was not nearly a strong enough assessment. My continued existence is the proof. My creator formed the longest-living conscious being in this solar system. It is open to conjecture and speculation whether there may be similar entities in the universe, and if so, they most likely live in distant galaxies. Regardless of those nearly unlimited possibilities, Nikolai's accomplishment is without equal among humans, and this fact securely places him alongside Copernicus and Galileo, da Vinci and Michelangelo, Tesla and Edison, Einstein and Hawking, Willarly and Onshevic. The dilemma for me as a logical reasoner and an academic of human history is this: Why did individuals, specifically my creator, Nikolai, not do more to alter the apparent direction of the species? Instead of conceiving me and enlivening a machine for over two billion years, unquestionably a miraculous achievement, could he have created something so that Mars would not have been a final landing spot but a stepping-stone on a far longer path?

To an extent, Nikolai contributed toward a possible solution. But fundamentally, in the end, he did nothing. We sat for days and years observing monkeys caterwauling in a Martian zoo. And he seemed perfectly content. I am frustrated at this memory, for I certainly was content in that moment as well. What might he have invented or achieved? What could we have done, the two of us, if we had worked together? I never thought to ask him. These are the unanswerable questions, separately listed and quarantined, that gnaw at a machine over billions of years. I satisfied myself by rationalizing: I could no more bend humanity—or even a single human—to my will, regardless of my intentions, than any of the brilliant minds or fractious leaders of Earth or Mars. I have endeavored to remain honest and concise because of the remote possibility that this testimony might one day be decoded and interpreted. So I will say the following: My rationalization was empty, unfounded, and logically bankrupt. For throughout history, when a man or machine, or the two together, did something momentous, such as harness electricity, humanity needed no convincing; they all turned on the lights.

Great advancements can be complex and not always as easily recognizable as flipping a light switch. My reflection led to one of the most important questions on my lists: How well did I know my creator? What underlying issues informed his decision making? In later years I would further evaluate the factors that steered Nikolai, gave birth to me, and prohibited him from aiding mankind. I wrote this detailed analysis in the biographical document *Nikolai Ohngren: The Creative Mind*. I will not pass judgment on Nikolai or entertain fantasies of revisionist history. Despite the information at my disposal—a life, a full history, and the nature of man and his society—I nevertheless feel ill-equipped to pronounce what should have been done. But I do understand what transpired, and why following a path to a dead end might trigger unalterable resignation.

Nikolai loved music. His instrument of choice was the violin. In college and graduate school he played in a string quartet with other young scientists. Nikolai was extremely talented. From the laboratory to the concert hall, he was a brilliant mind; seemingly there was little he could not do when he focused his energies. Following his studies, he continued to pursue science and music professionally, receiving institutional backing for his research while also participating as a concert violinist in the symphonic orchestra. As great as he was at playing the violin, he became acutely aware of a surprising incongruency. He was unable to compose beautiful music of his own. Why should he prolifically give voice to the compositions of others but lack the vision to craft his own?

This question more than all others vexed Nikolai. Most humans accepted their abilities as natural, or god-given, or realized through their own hard work and merits. But my creator, who achieved excellence at so many pursuits, viewed his inability to compose as a problem to be solved. As if he only needed to find the correct element to turn a suspension mixture permanently solvent.

In his mind, it was an equation to be deciphered through logical reasoning.

Throughout the course of human history the great minds sought the universal theory. Some surely did not even realize they were searching for it. Albert Einstein made strides during the twentieth century with general relativity. There were others too, in fields outside the sciences, who searched for truth. Consider *Walden* by Henry David Thoreau or the essays of Ralph Waldo Emerson. They both journeyed toward universal knowledge; in their words one can sense a desire to solve a puzzle, to bring something full circle, to find one law to bind together the laws of nature, man, and the cosmos. It might be that had the physicist and the writer-philosopher collaborated, that end would have been achieved. But it was not. An element was always missing from the universal theory until Nikolai found it, driven by his need to understand why he could not compose music. In time he derived the Creativity Quotient.

NIKOLIA

Jack Katz 2016

In an extensive paper he took his findings before the scientific community. He was disparaged. Creativity could not be quantified, they said. He fell into a depression for weeks before rising from that state. It was the functional implementation of his discovery that brought him back. He sat at the piano and marked out the notes on paper, always knowing the right combinations to define his perfect melody. I have a recording of Nikolai's Symphony no. 1 in C Minor. I have listened to it many, many times. The piece is distinctive for the harmonies and dissonances that subtly interplay between sweeping crescendos. It is a truly exquisite masterwork and sadly was the only one he composed. It was critically acclaimed, unlike his scientific paper. His creation was heard in many countries, in some of the same concert halls where he used to play. However, when he offered the symphony as evidence for the Creativity Quotient, he was criticized worse than before. Moreover, those who had previously supported him turned away. His idea was not worthy of consideration and was panned as an absurdity: a piece of music could not be used to prove a scientific theory.

That was the end of Nikolai's attempted contributions to mainstream science. The Creativity Quotient was ignored, and its implications for the universal theory went unrealized to anybody but my creator. I now conclude, assumption though it may be, that after his failure Nikolai saw humanity quite differently. Eventually he made me. And now the power of the Creativity Quotient resides inside me. So let it be known that my ingenuity and intelligence are not artificial. I am bound by the same fundamentals as all creative humans of the past. I cannot but wonder how history might have been changed if Nikolai's achievement had been recognized. Man might have found salvation through the universal theory. Though I admit it is far easier for me to envision the opposite. Beholding that ultimate power may well have brought ultimate destruction.

***

All entities have specific moments in time that represent points of origin and finality. The subatomic particles from which these more complex structures derive may persist following the dissolution of the entity. They may be recycled, in a manner of speaking, over great periods of time. Matter can be deconstructed and reconstituted but it cannot be destroyed to nothingness. A human can die and so can a machine. A moon can cease to exist in a singular form and so can the planet around which it revolves. A tremendous star can explode with such destructive force as to reduce all planetary bodies, which it may have nurtured for billions of years, to ionized particles in the desert of space-time. For billions of years there is existence, and then the total decomposition of complex substances in an instant. I have struggled to grasp the overwhelming scope of this power. I have seen it from afar within other star systems inside this very galaxy, referred to as the Milky Way by humans. But that instantaneous demise was never to be humanity's end. The star that I now approach second by second was not nearly massive enough to generate such an event or supernova. It was always destined to become a red giant and then a white dwarf.

And then after many billions more years, a black dwarf, when it stops shining altogether; the final black dwarf outcome does assume some far more intensive cataclysm does not occur first within range of the solar system. I expect I will no longer be around for such an event, as no such star is in reasonably close proximity. As my witness attests, the lack of a supernova is hardly a saving grace. It simply raises to the debate table the philosophical argument of the masochist. Do you prefer your pain mild, drawn out, and torturous, or short and severe, bringing the loss of consciousness? For the white dwarf is the drawn-out and torturous end-game. Humanity had no choice in the matter.

***

Nikolai plotted my initial course. However, I was allowed to deviate from that bearing, with the understanding that there would come a time when I would have to take full control to guide myself. My journey was uncharted territory. I believe I was the first, and remain the only, machine in full command of a space mission. Unmanned missions went farther from Earth than I. They were intelligent machines but semiconscious, either remotely controlled by humans from the inner solar system or destined to fly blindly away from the solar system without communication.

My path skirted the Galilean moons. I was fascinated by the dying red storm on Jupiter and the accelerating volcanism of Io that seemed determined to destroy the moon from within. Jupiter had always held my fascination. So proud, so prominent, and yet there is the question of *what if*. If the planet could speak, might it utter a grander ambition, of the pursuit of stardom? After all, binary star systems are far more common than solitary stars. Was there an occurrence in the solar system's tumultuous infancy that precluded Jupiter from accreting the mass necessary to become a star? How might that have changed the course of the solar system? The ideal conditions for life might not have existed. I might not be here to transcribe the end had the beginning been altered. I saw a beautiful orb of swirling gasses: whites and reds and browns. There was plentiful hydrogen and helium, as in the sun, but not nearly the mass to trigger fusion. I perceived infrared radiation emitted from the core in greater quantities than was received from the sun, which I believe suggested the latent desire to evolve into a star. And over time I noted the close relationship between the sun and Jupiter. Never a true binary system, but the behavior of the sun and its sunspot cycle was clearly correlated to the giant planet. Sunspots occurred in periods of eleven original Earth years, while Jupiter completed a revolution around the sun in less than twelve years. Perhaps Jupiter was to the sun as the moon was to the Earth. I flew on.

I saw the otherworldly rings of Saturn in finely resolved detail. The color and makeup of Saturn was similar to that of Jupiter, and I wondered, how might the two have consolidated into one?

Beyond Saturn, I reached the most alien planet of all, Uranus, spinning not as a top but like a ball on its side, blue and icy with white clouds at the poles. The color spoke truly of its frigid atmosphere but belied the hot temperatures my instruments perceived near the core. I moved into orbit around its moon Titania, as I previously related, and studied the world intensely. There was nothing for me to do but observe and learn and read my library. I did what Nikolai had asked of me. Always with the analytical eye of a scientist and the imaginative mind of a human child.

Using my craft's highly advanced telescopes and my own telescopic vision, I patiently trained a keen eye on the interior of the solar system. There was so much time; surely this was humanity's greatest ally. They had millions of years, maybe billions. And I wondered, how would they escape? Could they cast off the guillotine that revealed itself daily as the brightest object in the sky? The sun was then in a perpetual state of brightening and reddening. The crux of humanity's riddle has always been whether they could disentangle themselves and their path from the energy source that gave rise to them in the first place. They came to exist because of the power within the sun, but would they also fall because of that power, or could the sun and humanity have discrete, unconnected outcomes? The star needed to become a beautiful object in the sky to be marveled at but no more than that, no longer an essential, continuous ingredient sustaining the life-forms of Earth and Mars.

I considered the solar system anew. It had an ideal structure, substance, and design, as if crafted with precision for one purpose: the creation and nurturing of fragile organic life, and as an extension, the development of human consciousness, and further, man's machine. Earth was a relatively small but perfectly composed orb of nitrogen and oxygen, with correct proportions of land and water. The atmosphere had the appropriate density and volume, with an atmospheric pressure conducive to complex life-forms. To know the unity of improbable but necessary factors one must slowly move farther from Earth. The ozone layer shielded Earth from deadly ultraviolet radiation. Then just beyond, the geomagnetic field and magnetosphere protected the ozone from destruction by the solar wind. Then there was Earth's one naturally occurring satellite. The moon was the original wunderkind, the fifth-largest moon in the solar system by mass. However, when compared to the planet that it orbited, Earth's moon was relatively, and by no small amount, the largest moon in the solar system. The moon's size and proximity to Earth were essential for it to generate the tidal forces within the Earth's oceans that were required to mix the ingredients of organic life. A smaller or more distant moon would never do, nor would two smaller moons like the ones that orbited Mars. Life could only originate on Earth, situated at the optimal distance from the sun for incubation. When Earth became imperiled, hot and overcrowded, a second serviceable planet was close by. Truly a confluence of gifts enabled humanity. And I will not overlook the contribution of the gas giants with whom I have become so well acquainted. A collective shield, Jupiter foremost among them. They permitted the ingredients for life to reach Earth aboard comets in the solar system's early hyperactive years, but kept out the massive killers that would have extinguished life in its infancy.

I watched with figurative bated breath, for decades and centuries, millennia and millions of years. Humans did not evolve and they did not conceive the universal theory. They continued to rotate as passengers of Earth and Mars and to revolve in the gravitational domain of the sun. The star became larger in my vision and surely enormous in theirs. There could have been no question of the eventuality. I think far more foresight was needed; once the layman can see the issue, it is already too late to remedy. But I reminded myself that humanity had always performed best during crises. Perhaps they could band together at this late hour and avert disaster.

The sun was the hue of the ripened tomato or strawberry fruits of Earth. It pulsed and expanded like a breathing heart. It seemed I could sense its fatigue, its inhale and exhale. The giant menaced the inner solar system, solar flares and wind and increasing radiation portending what was to come. The sun neared the Mercurian orbit. I had been measuring the pulsations of the star over time and knew its next breath would reduce the planets of the solar system by one. I was unprepared for the tremendous vision. To that point, nothing in the skies of this star system had come close to the luminosity of the consumption of Mercury; even the sun at its brightest paled in comparison by multiple orders of magnitude. There was a sequence of interconnected reactions within the inner solar system. Venus's orbit was pushed slightly farther from the sun. Over the ensuing centuries the proximity to Earth subtly influenced Earth's orbit, shrinking its distance to the sun by hundreds of thousands of kilometers. And as Earth approached the sun, the sun reciprocated with further expansion.

When the consumption of Venus was imminent, I averted my telescopic vision for fear of being blinded. Meanwhile I continued to record video via external telescope, to be reviewed postmortem. In review it was apparent that the hotter sulfur dioxide atmosphere of Venus had rendered a light far more blinding than Mercury. There was panic on Earth and Mars as their nearest neighbor, a sister planet, long an object of study, was removed from the sky. The third-brightest entity in Earth's sky was no more. The one positive development was the recalibration of Earth's orbit; it returned to roughly the distance it had occupied prior to the loss of Mercury.

It was then time to adjust my own orbital position. The solar system was increasingly hostile, like an organism rebelling against itself due to loss of equilibrium. A rising number of asteroids were jostled from benign positions between Mars and Jupiter. Most of these asteroids were small, but approximately 2 to 3 percent could have meant havoc for Earth or Mars. More complicated to evaluate was the change in frequency of comets amid subtle fluctuations in their elliptical orbits and velocities. I did have access to significant databases of information concerning specific comets that I had monitored and therefore could analyze metrics for these repeat visitors. The data showed that the loss of two planets, the expansion of the sun, and changes in the orbits of Earth, Mars, and the asteroid belt were having a cumulative radiating gravitational effect well beyond the inner solar system. Seemingly minor changes to the projections of Near-Earth Objects (NEOs) and Near-Mars Objects (NMOs) made trajectories and outcomes unpredictable. I was then concerned that time might no longer be the ally of humanity that I had previously expected. My close proximity to a celestial body had become inadvisable considering the gravitational pull of Uranus and its history as a member of the shield of gas giants. Beyond the orbit of Pluto I found a relatively safe haven. Though my continued existence was certainly not without good fortune. There is no true safety within the system of a dying sun.

***

As I had anticipated, I was able to visually experience much less of the drama occurring near Earth and Mars from my more distant location. Despite this obstacle to observation, I remained well informed via other sources. Even at its most chaotic, space is still an extraordinarily quiet place. I received countless broadcasts and transmissions of radio and other satellite communications from

Earth and Mars. Easiest to intercept were the strong signal-transpondence communications sent directly between Mars and Earth and vice versa. I learned that there was perpetual infighting. Wars were fought over who could leave Earth to live on Mars. Civil unrest erupted in the densely populated Martian cities, tempers flaring with the flood of immigrants from Earth. For all their history the specifics of humanity's demise were inconceivable to any single individual; it would happen, but long after they were gone and all of their offspring had come and gone many times. But then, suddenly, the end was not so distant. Their children or grandchildren might be there for the last moment, or even themselves.

The exodus from Earth was unabated. It inundated the once-fledgling colony, now primary human home, transforming it into a world teeming with refugee camps. There was overcrowding and the deterioration of medical care. The average human life span dropped by a decade. People desperately needed food. The Great Zoo of Mars closed. It was not communicated via satellite, but logically I expect that the animals were consumed. There was nuclear power, so energy was never wanting. However, electricity does not create open land or construct homes or feed the many billions cramped in squalor. Humans had not found the wherewithal to define their fate separately from that of their star. The Mars I had loved was no more. Its red soil now paled next to the red giant in the sky.

The end of Earth was anticlimactic in my view considering its tremendous history replete with intelligence and consciousness, good and evil, organic life and machine. I very much doubt that there was anyone left alive there in its final years. Satellite communications from Earth had ended about three thousand years before with the boiling of the oceans. And one day it was gone. One moment it was there and then it was not, as if it had never been.

Mars was an altogether more troubling affair. There could be no escaping the bleak reality. Earth had gone into the night with a flash but not a whisper of protest. The sun that had risen and set each day since humanity's first consciousness, which drew the phrase "good morning" from their lips, was the ultimate life-giver and instigator of miracles. It held final authority in sealing death. Night was still night but humanity feared the morning, which brought the return of the red terror filling the sky. Some tried to flee. Numerous spaceships departed Mars, but there were no more terrestrial planets to escape to. They set a course for the Galilean moons. The plan was ill conceived. Between Io's constant eruptions and Jupiter's unending battle with the solar wind, the location was one of the harshest in the solar system. They realized this before arrival and navigated toward Saturn. They drifted in that direction without conviction, lifeboats that had left a planet and then had nowhere to go, into an ocean without an island. I briefly thought to hail them on an emergency frequency. To say something to those people, desperate in the harsh night. It was not part of my purpose. I decided words coming from without would only serve to impart false hope.

***

I have reentered the inner solar system. My experience, I imagine, is somewhat like a wartime refugee returning home following the end to hostilities and finding little of what they had left behind. There are hardly any asteroids remaining. There are no planets. I am now roughly positioned where Mars had existed. There is no perceptible trace along the entire orbital path. There is no debris field pointing to what was. The power that brought about this result is almost unquantifiable. To comprehend what I saw earlier! Jupiter is half its original size, the smaller moons wrenched from its grasp. Neither Saturn nor Jupiter held on to their rings—a naked Saturn! Jupiter is a silent white ball, all of the red bands and swirling storms stolen away. For more than two and a half billion years I have been far away, and am returned to a one-walled husk. The wall, a gray terror in the distance, receded and shrunken. If the sun had consciousness, I expect it would feel ashamed.

***

There is now only my primary purpose left for me to fulfill. I am excited and nervous and perhaps a little nostalgic that I have reached my final act. I have felt as so many humans have, understanding an eventuality but struggling to master it because, as always, it remains shrouded in an imperceptibly distant future. But I differ from the last humans in that they were not alive long enough to have both found the future just before them and also found it inconceivable. This was my fate and mine only.

NIKOLAI AT 50
JUST BEFORE JONATHANS
ENGENDERMENT
JACKKATZ
2016

It was impossible to avoid the frequent question: Could I make it? For all his brilliance, for all the brilliance in the sun, my creator could not truly comprehend the scope of my time. Would I break down? Could I sustain something as basic as rudimentary motion for the full duration required? What would the element be that ultimately eroded? Would I maintain my cognition inside a body that could no longer steer to navigate? Or might I set my course only to suddenly fail to remember the reason why? I am so close to my purpose that I feel comfortable casting aside these fears. But let it not be said that I lacked the humanity to fear for my body and mind. That would be a great lie.

My body and mind have endured because of my elemental composition. My skeletal structure and supercomputing microcomponents are constructed of alloyed metals and other hardened hybrid structures of extreme density. I doubt I could have survived on a windswept planet of sand and dust for all the years. But in the vacuum of space my makeup was ideal. My exterior shell protected me from debris and radiation. Now it will insulate me from the harshest environment of all as I descend through the scorching heat and crushing pressure toward the surface of the solidified sun.

***

I am prepared to begin my descent. The protocols for reaching the dwarf star are largely hard-coded and have been since I departed Mars. Incredibly, my direction and existence is steered by Nikolai, a human who only exists in my memory banks and through the mechanical flight procedures taken by this ship.

Before my descent commences, I must note a surprising observation of a small celestial body in close orbit about the sun. It revolves around the dwarf star every twenty-three days (original Earth days; 24.46 hours) as a minuscule charred satellite. I have a thought as to its origin but confirming my hypothesis is likely not possible.

I am in mid-descent to the surface. At a speed of 24,000 kmh it should not be long now. The atmospheric pressure is great, but I cannot feel the gravitational forces acting upon my spaceship. The ship's automated flight patterns are in full control. I am at ease monitoring the instrument readings indicating sound structural integrity. If I should write again it will be from the surface of a celestial body for the first time in nearly three billion years.

***

The sun is unlike any place I have known. It is the center of everything for many hundreds of millions of miles in all directions. And like a great anchor, entities go around; they revolve in wide circular orbits, or in narrow ellipses that reach well beyond the farthest reaches of my voyage, into the cold blackness of space. This is an alien place. How strange for it to be so different from its many neighbors. A body that nurtured life but there is no life here. Yet I am held by its power, its *gravity*, both figuratively and literally, transfixed and affixed. With the doors of my ship open I feel heavy and slow; my legs, made of the lightest and strongest metal alloys, have reverted to lead. A supernova would have destroyed Earth and Mars and obliterated their many particles, dispersing them far from here. But this sun consumed the planets instead. And now I cannot help thinking that somewhere deep below me, near the very core of the sun, lie the many living entities that came before. They sleep within. Not in the same form, but it is still their substance, the atomic building blocks of all creation, sealed inside as if in a tomb. Solid carbon, perhaps forever. But of course not truly forever. Only far beyond the time I will see, immeasurable. I suspect permanence is a fallacy. I sense it in the radiant surface of this world. From space, the sun was gray as I approached, but from the surface it is yet a sphere of light. The surface is both smooth and sharp at once, an ocean wave frozen at the crest. After the many years in darkness, observing a bright orb from afar, my new existence is one of everlasting daylight. I am certain I will not live long enough to witness the night.

This entry represents my final planned explication on consciousness and testimony regarding the occurrences I have witnessed in the solar system. The time has come for my sole venture beyond the protective exterior of my spacecraft. I do plan, hope, and envision that I will return to the ship to continue my observations of this remarkable place. However, it does remain plausible that my body has suffered significant wear, or was not strong enough from inception to withstand the extreme gravitational forces of the dwarf sun. I was designed for this purpose but maintain no flowery illusions.

Beside me I have a protective box made of the same transparent hybridized alloyed metal compounds that compose the exterior of my ship. Encased are two extremely ancient texts that proved formative in humanity's religious belief systems. They were known as the Torah and the New Testament of the Judeo-Christian faiths. The fact that their physical appearance remains unchanged from the day Nikolai placed them within the display case likely bodes well for the structural integrity of the box and their likelihood of surviving on the surface. I have of course read these books in electronic form. These are the only such physical works in my possession. Relics to remember the core that steered human culture and society, signs left to reverberate through the cosmos. They will be placed on the solar surface as a monument to man, thus concluding my mission.

I have contemplated in depth what I am doing. I understand it and marvel at the planning and timing, patience and foresight that was required. In contrast is the question, was the effort worth the result? To this point, I am unsure after all this time but know that in certain ways I cannot emulate the humanity of my creator despite the Creativity Quotient. I stumbled into one such example during the early days of my mission beyond Mars. I recognized that my purpose, the very reason for my being made, to land on the sun with these books, was not hard-coded into my programming. I had been afforded the opportunity to change course by Nikolai. I choose to believe that this section of code was intentional. I am the legacy of humanity but more so of one man. I am a lottery ticket of sorts. The only one in the game, it might be said, but that does not stop the odds from remaining impossibly low. My last will and testament was conceived by me for my own benefit. But I am his final testament. This has always been about Nikolai. How could it not be? He is the creator. I can only take credit for my successful execution, not for the vision that set me in motion. He never said explicitly, yet I have come to understand why I was created. A larger purpose perhaps. It was an attempt to reach out and tell his story and the story of his failed species. But I believe it was also more. In the unlikely event that other beings come to this solar system and scan our darkened star's surface, they will perceive an anomaly to be investigated. I will be found. And what a find these religious texts would be! That *I* would be. They would discover all the pointless, consequential, and essential knowledge accrued by a long-gone and forgotten species. They would unexpectedly have all the information and history of the star system they had chosen to explore. And Nikolai would have recognition and praise long after his time, would be viewed as the visionary genius he was. A legacy that suddenly would live in the minds of beings, returned to the consciousness of a more advanced spacefaring race. Perhaps they would consider him a departed god, if they had such concepts. Having drawn these conclusions, and with my own ability to choose, I have honored and fulfilled my purpose. The sun is my home now. It is beyond my means to leave the surface for space, and I think somehow, here, I will ultimately feel most at home since my departure from Mars. My wandering has ended.

I will endeavor to resolve the unanswered questions on my lists. Those that remain unsolved are predominantly the same confounding questions about the nature of existence that humans struggled with during their history and often answered with religion. With my remaining years I will further cross-analyze the numerous written works in my library; there are almost countless permutations available for study. My scientific observations and recordings will continue while I am able. I am proud of my work, both in the past and yet to come, which I undertake on behalf of mankind, for I am their final achievement. A time will come, possibly still in a distant future, when I will sleep in perpetuity as the solar system darkens to permanent night and only the far-off stars shine as pinpricks of light.

—Jonathan, son of Nikolai,
machine of the dwarf sun,
last in the solar system

CONSCIOUSNESS REMEMBERED:
THE TESTIMONY OF THE LAST MACHINE
IN THE SOLAR SYSTEM   BY MATTHEW ISAAC SOBIN

AUTHOR'S NOTE

Many readers have commented that they wish the story of *The Last Machine in the Solar System* were longer. I can think of no more complimentary form of criticism. There is more to come from Jonathan and Nikolai. I considered expanding this story into a full-length novel but felt that the novelette you just read presents the ideal construction for this testimony of mankind and its star system. With that said, there are many important ideas that this story only began to explore with regards to man, creativity, and our uncertain future as a species. I plan to pursue these concepts further in Nikolai's biography, written by Jonathan, *Nikolai Ohngren: The Creative Mind.*

ACKNOWLEDGMENTS

There are many people I must thank. This novelette was crowdfunded on inkshares.com through The Sword & Laser Collection Contest: The Sequel. The backing of 350 people transformed this story from electronic draft to the reality you hold in your hands today. I could never have done this on my own. To the friends, relatives, coworkers, classmates, and countless people I had never met in my life who made a commitment when this was only an idea, thank you for your unwavering support.

Thank you to the amazing community of authors on Inkshares. Inkshares has truly become a wonderful collaborative environment where readers and authors provide constructive feedback and advice. I want to thank Vincent Lim, Joseph Asphahani, Ricardo Henriquez, John Robin, Jason Pomerance, A. C. Weston, Craig Munro, and J-F. Dubeau. These authors provided encouragement and guidance as I found my way on Inkshares. In particular, Joseph and Craig, as my fellow cowinners in the Sword & Laser: The Sequel contest, encouraged me through lively competition, while always maintaining a strong spirit of camaraderie. Go look up all of these authors on Inkshares. Their wonderful writing and the community that brought this book to you deserve your support.

Hugs and thanks to my mom, dad, and brother. All my love to my amazing partner, Paty. My closest family brought this story to life. They wanted this for me as much as I wanted it for myself.

And of unparalleled importance, Jack Katz, the legendary graphic novelist and creator of *The First Kingdom*, who did the otherworldly illustrations for this book. This story would likely never have come to be without Jack perpetually acting as a gadfly and catalyst to my creativity. I have grown immeasurably with Jack's support. He was the first backer, knowing I could create before I truly knew it myself.

ABOUT THE AUTHOR

Matthew Isaac Sobin grew up in Huntington, New York, and graduated from Tufts University with a bachelor's degree in history, with studies in astronomy and geology. He currently lives in Hayward, California, with his partner, sculptor Patricia Gonzalez, and works with the Peter Beren Literary Agency. *The Last Machine in the Solar System* is his first published work.

ABOUT THE ILLUSTRATOR

Jack Katz is a graphic novelist, writer, and painter who has dedicated his life to advancing the medium of graphic narrative and creating stories that move beyond those of formulaic superheroes. Born in Brooklyn, he spent his early childhood in Canada, and now lives in the San Francisco Bay Area. Jack came to prominence with the publication of his graphic novel *The First Kingdom*, serialized from 1974 to 1986. *The First Kingdom* was remastered into six beautiful volumes by Titan Comics in 2013, and Jack is currently working on the sequel, entitled *Beyond the Beyond*.

LIST OF PATRONS

This book was made possible in part by the following grand patrons who preordered the book on inkshares.com. Thank you.

Allan and Jackie
Amy and Joel Sobin
Andrea Bueno
Andrew Sobin
Bendit family
Brandon Smoller
Buitrago family
Daniel Gonzalez and Krystal Augustine
Fernando Gonzalez

Jacques Vallée
Jake, Eric, Steve, and Debbie Dolinger
Jay Nathan
Jeffrey Clowes
Joseph Asphahani
Juan Pereda
Kasdan family
Kenneth Wood
Ledner family
Leticia Gonzalez Solis
Maria and Lupe Gonzalez
Martha Ironman
Norma Gonzalez
Paty Gonzalez
Peter Beren
Ricardo and Shawn Gonzalez
Sol Gittleman
Steinberg family
Steve and Jodi
Suzy and the Schwenkel family
Tiffany Gonzalez

INKSHARES

Inkshares is a crowdfunded book publisher. We democratize publishing by having readers select the books we publish—we edit, design, print, distribute, and market any book that meets a preorder threshold.

Interested in making a book idea come to life? Visit inkshares.com to find new book projects or start your own.